D1564766

PARARESCUE CORPS

BY MICHAEL P. SPRADLIN
ILLUSTRATED BY SPIROS KARKAVELAS

STONE ARCH BOOKS
a capstone imprint

SANDSTORM BLAST

A 4D BOOK

Pararescue Corps is published by
Stone Arch Books, A Capstone Imprint
1710 Roe Crest Drive
North Mankato, Minnesota 56003
www.mycapstone.com

Library of Congress Cataloging-in-Publication Data
is available on the Library of Congress website.
ISBN: 978-1-4965-5159-7 (Library Binding)
ISBN: 978-1-4965-5204-4 (eBookPDF)

Editor: Hank Musolf
Designer: Ted Williams
Production: Laura Manthe

Design Elements:

Shutterstock: John T Takai, MicroOne

Printed and bound in Canada.
PA020

Download the Capstone app!

- Ask an adult to download the Capstone 4D app.

- Scan the cover and stars inside the book for additional content.

When you scan a spread, you'll find
fun extra stuff to go with this book!
You can also find these things
on the web at www.capstone4D.com
using the password: blast.51597

TABLE OF CONTENTS

◎ CHAPTER 1

The word came down quietly and quickly to the fighters in the valley. It was time to move out. The Americans, in their cozy base near the village below, had a curious custom. Each morning all the men in the compound staffed their stations in full battle gear. The Americans called it "Stand To," short for "Standing to Arms."

It would be different today, here in the Shashim valley. Today the Americans would pay. To Malik it meant that they expected an attack. They wanted to show the Taliban that they were always ready. At this hour, troops were falling in for Stand To in American bases all over Afghanistan. They expected an attack that seldom came.

It would be different today, here in the Shashim valley. Today the Americans would pay.

Today Americans would die.

Malik hefted his rifle, slinging it around his shoulder. Together with his partner, Abdul, they lifted the crate and stepped silently down the goat trail. The crate contained rockets for the rocket-propelled grenade, or RPG. There were nearly four hundred well-armed fighters in the hills above the village this morning.

The American base sat about three hundred yards from the village. There was a concrete bunker at the rear of the compound. A wall of sandbags circled it. Barbed wire coiled around the sandbags on the outside. No doubt the Americans had placed Claymore mines among the barbed wire. They had built a reasonable defensive position in a short amount of time.

The leader of this attack was named Nassar. He was a seasoned Taliban fighter. During the Iraq War he trained with Al Qaeda in Afghanistan. As they sat by the fire last night, Abdul mentioned that Nassar had fought with Bin Laden against the Russians. Nassar was a hard man and battle tested. Their confidence was high as they crept down the hills toward their enemy.

"We must not lose our place," Abdul said quietly. Someone up ahead shushed him. He was glad it was dark. Abdul would not see his angry face. He and Abdul were among the youngest people on this mission.

Mistakes would not be tolerated. Abdul was clumsy and oafish. They must be silent. Abdul loved to talk. Right now, Malik wanted Abdul to love carrying crates in silence.

The crate was heavy. It wouldn't be good if it went tumbling down the mountain, alerting everyone to their presence. Each step they took was carefully measured.

A week ago, the Americans arrived and began building their base. The soldiers hired local workers to help in the construction. It was an ideal situation for Nassar. He could send in spies to pose as workers. They soon told him everything about the Americans and their position. It was priceless information. For example, he'd learned they had constructed a strong concrete bunker.

Good to know.

He would not waste more than token energy on trying to destroy it. He also discovered the Americans only had one mortar. They would have to call for air support or artillery from their main base nearly an hour away. If the attack unfolded as planned, they could keep the Americans out of touch long enough to ensure a victory.

Now there was a storm coming. Nassar's forces were far more agile than the soldiers crammed into the base. They knew the terrain. The sound of the storm would cover their approach. Everything was moving in their favor. Allahu Akbar. God is great.

Malik's stomach growled. It was three days since he'd had anything more than some bread crust. He was constantly hungry. It was a large part of the reason he joined the Taliban. Most of the time they had food. When they didn't, Malik and the other fighters were told they were suffering for Allah. Malik believed even Allah would want his soldiers to be fed. Malik knew Abdul and some of the other boys his age joined because they wanted to make Holy War. To bring jihad to the west. Malik was a believer in their mission. But mostly he just wanted to eat.

Afghanistan had been at war since he was a child. He was born in the capital city of Kabul. His father was forced to fight and die by a Taliban warlord when Malik was very young. Then his mother passed from an illness. Malik had no brothers or sisters. For a while his aunt took him in. But her family was pressed for money and had little to offer an orphan—even one who was a family member.

After that, everything in his life had fallen apart. He stopped going to school. Eventually he was sleeping on the streets. There was a group of boys he ran with who found food at a mosque in a broken-down neighborhood of western Kabul. The Iman, the clergy man who ran the mosque, gave them odd jobs and more food when it was available. The odd jobs eventually turned into spying.

As a group of homeless kids, they had the perfect cover. They could run the streets, watching the convoys and other vehicles. On the fields near the base, they watched as replacement units arrived. The new soldiers replaced those who had been "in country" for at least a year. This was important information. New units were composed of scared, fresh-out-of-basic-training troops.

The order to halt was quietly transmitted up the line. It was still dark. The cloud cover omitted the moon. Malik and Abdul carefully set the crate down. As their eyes adjusted to the darkness, they looked for a spot that would offer them cover. A fighter with the RPG launcher appeared out of the darkness.

"Can you reload?" he whispered to Malik.

"Yes," Malik answered.

"And you," he said to Abdul, "you can run for some more ammunition?"

"Yes," Abdul said.

"Good. Be ready. Allahu Akbar," the man said.

The entire mountainside grew quiet. There were no bird noises. No sounds from insects. Even the wind had died down.

The seconds ticked by. They were a good 300 meters from the base. Still, they could hear the noises of the soldiers moving about in the darkness. They waited. And waited. With dawn approaching, the sounds of the soldiers retreated. They slipped back into their shelters, Stand To over. The man holding the RPG tapped Malik on the arm. Malik removed an RPG from the crate and loaded it into the launcher. The man raised it to his shoulder and aimed carefully.

They waited. Sweat formed along Malik's forehead. After a few more minutes, Malik wondered if the attack had been called off. The man's cell phone vibrated in his pocket.

Then the air and sky were filled with fire.

◎ CHAPTER 2

Location: Forward Operating Base Falcon,
          Shashim Valley, Kunar Province,
          Afghanistan
Date: August 14th
Time: 0600 hours

Bullets zipped into the dirt around Chief Master Sergeant Gregory "Mako" Marks. The ground shook. Rocks and chunks of dirt flew everywhere. Mako covered his patient with his own body.

"RPG incoming!" Airman Ahmad Bashir shouted. A few seconds later, the rocket exploded thirty yards away. They barely had time to brace for it.

Mako was surrounded by noise and confusion.

They were at FOB Falcon in the Shashim Valley of Afghanistan. The Taliban and other terrorist factions were stepping up attacks in this part of the country. This morning a large group launched an offensive on the base. There were just over forty soldiers staffing FOB Falcon. Fighting against three or four hundred terrorists, they were severely outnumbered. They had been fighting for a half hour when Mako and the Air Force Pararescuemen, or PJs, showed up.

Mako tried to tune out the distractions. "Blood pressure is ninety over forty," Bashir said.

"Ten ccs of adrenaline," Mako said.

Bashir administered the medicine through the IV.

The soldier's name was Washington. He had a bullet wound to the head. The right side of his face was covered in blood. Unconscious, he was in critical condition. They needed to stabilize him and get him evacuated quickly.

"Blood pressure rising," Bashir said. "One hundred ten over seventy."

Mako looked up to the sky above them. Two Pave Hawk helicopters, Pedro One and Pedro Two, circled the battlefield. Each chopper used its .50 caliber machine gun to return fire on the enemy. They were going to have to lower the rescue basket to save private Washington.

It was incredibly dangerous. The helicopter had to hover in place for several minutes while the patient was lifted aboard. It made a tempting target. They needed a diversion to keep the enemy quiet while they moved their patients.

"Lieutenant?" Mako said into his radio.

"I'm here, Mako," Lieutenant Jamal Jenkins said.

Jenkins was the team CRO, Combat Rescue Officer. His voiced cracked and faded. The radio connections were spotty. He was back at airfield Thorsness coordinating the mission. Jenkins was an excellent CRO. But Mako knew at that moment he really wanted to be on the ground with his men.

"Any chance at an air strike?" Mako asked.

"I've got two A-10s inbound right now," Jenkins said. "They should be there in three minutes."

"Excellent," Mako said. "Bash, let's get him ready to go. Pedro Two, do you read me?"

"Loud and clear, Mako," Technical Sergeant Jose Garcia said.

Garcia and Master Sergeant Frank George were aboard Pedro Two. They were eager for their turn to help get the injured soldier to safety.

"Get ready. We've got air support coming," Mako said. "We're going to send him up right after the A-10s do their thing. Hopefully the air strike will keep the bad guys quiet long enough. Be on standby."

"Standing by," Garcia said.

Mako checked his watch. "Heads up," Mako said. "Stay ready to deploy basket, everyone. We are thirty-seven minutes, repeat three-seven minutes into the

Golden Hour. Garcia, when you get him on board, hustle back to the base."

"Will do, Sarge," Garcia said over the radio.

The Golden Hour was the first hour after a patient was wounded. Every effort possible was made to get them to the base hospital within an hour. If they were successful, the patient had a much better chance of survival. The Golden Hour was tracked very carefully during the mission.

The air filled with the roar of aircraft engines.

Mako looked to the east. Two A-10 Warthogs appeared on the horizon. They were flying at 400 miles per hour. The A-10 jet plane carried a huge, .30mm, seven-barrel Gatling gun in its nose. The gun could fire almost 4,000 times in a minute. It also carried powerful missiles. It could do a lot of damage.

They flew in overhead like two angry ravens. Missiles streaked from their wings north of their position into the mountainside. Mako and Bashir shielded private Washington's body with their own. The roar and dust from the A-10 attacks faded. As soon as they cleared the area, Pedro Two hovered into position. The basket plunged down from the chopper.

The air strike had disoriented the attackers. But

slowly, the gunfire returned. Mako and Bashir loaded Washington into the basket. It started up slowly. The enemies fired at it.

"Go! Go! GO!" Mako shouted as he watched the basket climb.

The men could hear bullets bouncing off its sides. Sparks flew as it climbed closer to the chopper.

It seemed to take hours, but the basket was secured in Pedro Two in a few seconds. The chopper banked away, climbing in altitude. In a few more seconds it was a speck on the horizon as it zoomed back to the airfield. Pedro One's crew followed to refuel and wait for further instructions. It was forty-nine minutes into the Golden Hour. There wasn't much time left.

Mako slumped back against the sandbags lining their position. Bashir sat next to him.

"Smith? Where are you?" Mako said into the radio. Another senior airman on the team, Phil Smith, had fast-roped down to treat wounded along with Bashir. Mako and Bashir tended to Private Washington while Smith went off to examine the others that were injured. He was also the team's sniper. Mako wondered if he'd found a place he could set up his rifle.

"Smith! Respond," Mako said.

Smith did not answer.

"You suppose his radio is busted?" Bashir asked.

"Could be. But I don't like it," Mako said. "This position has been taking almost nonstop fire."

The enemy had recovered from the A-10 air strike. Machine gun fire and RPGs rained down on the base.

"How did we get here, sarge?" Bashir asked.

"It's how we roll, airman," Mako said.

"What are we going to do?" Bashir asked.

Mako picked up his M-4 rifle leaning against the wall of sandbags.

"Bash," Mako said. "If we don't have to fix theem, then we'll just fight with them. At least until our ride gets here."

"Roger that, sarge," Bashir said.

Off to the west, the wind grew stronger. A storm gathered strength. Sand pelted the rocks and trees like tiny bullets. The constant stream of swirling air moved over the ground like a giant snowplow.

It was headed straight toward the Shashim Valley.

◎ CHAPTER 3

Location: Air Base Thorsness,
         Kunar Province, Afghanistan
Date: August 14th
Time: 0700 hours

The sky darkened to the west of the base. Huge clouds blew toward them. The wind was sharp. It carried sand from the dessert. Lieutenant Jamal Jenkins had been in the medical center for two hours. He had watched and directed Mako and the other PJs on their mission to FOB Falcon. Now the two Pave Hawks had returned with the wounded soldier, and he was safely in the hospital.

Every second counted. The storm was going to play havoc with flight operations. If it got bad enough, they wouldn't even be able to go out in ground vehicles. Not with zero visibility.

Jenkins had called in a request for two evac helicopters. They were also Pave Hawks, just bigger. With any luck they could evacuate the entire air base. Regardless, Jenkins intended to have all his people on board that chopper when it lifted off.

He heard the incoming chopper pilots on the radio. They were on their approach. He grabbed his rifle and ruck and headed out to the tarmac. The big aircraft were just touching down. He was met by Garcia and George.

"What's the story, Loot?" Garcia asked over the roar of the engines.

"We're going back to FOB Falcon," Jenkins said. "Going to evacuate the base if we can. Provide support if we can't."

"Roger that," George said.

They followed their Lieutenant and climbed aboard the big Pave Hawk. The choppers took on extra fuel and more ammo. Then they lifted off. It was a fifteen-minute flight to FOB Falcon.

It was a rough ride. The leading edge of the storm was upon them. The wind stiffened. Jenkins, Garcia, and George were quiet as the choppers pushed through the stiff air.

"Five minutes out," the pilot said over the intercom.

"What's the situation on the ground?" Garcia asked.

"No update," Jenkins said. "The storm is causing trouble with communications. There's no new information since you guys were there."

"Why is it we can't get radios to work in a storm?"

George asked. "I mean Denali, here. You'd think they'd be coming up with some tougher radios by now."

"I think it's because they keep trying to make everything smaller," said Jenkins. "You make tiny stuff, it can't stand up to anything. We need radios like they carried back in the day. With a backpack. That would solve it."

The Pave Hawks flew over FOB Falcon from the west. To avoid taking fire as much as possible, they planned to land to the south with the compound between them and the village. The village, nothing more than a collection of houses and two-story buildings, was where most of the fire was coming from.

The chopper jerked in the air. Without warning, it spun wildly in the air. The pilot struggled to maintain control. "We're hit! We're hit!" the pilot shouted. "Brace for impact!"

The chopper spun through the air, trailing smoke. "Dead stick! Dead stick!" the pilot shouted. It twisted through the sky toward the mountains east of the village. The pilot tried in vain to regain control.

"Hang on!" Jenkins said.

The Pave Hawk gained speed. The ground rushed up to meet it. It broke apart and shattered nearly a kilometer away from the compound—crashing right in the middle of the terrorist forces.

◎ CHAPTER 4

Location: FOB Falcon, Shashim Valley,
          Kunar Province, Afghanistan
Date: August 14th
Time: 0710 hours

A whistling sound meant they only had a split second to act.

"Get down! Incoming!" A young sergeant named Henderson crouched next to Mako and Bashir.

They slumped behind a wall of sandbags. Mako tried to make his giant body as small as possible. It wasn't easy. An explosion rocked the ground. Dirt and shrapnel flew everywhere.

"You guys okay?" Henderson asked.

"Yeah. I guess they haven't run out of ammunition," Mako said.

Sergeant Henderson carried an M-240, which was a combination machine gun and grenade launcher. To Mako, the young sergeant dressed in battle armor looked like some ancient warrior—like a Roman or Spartan soldier who knew nothing else but combat.

The sergeant thought Mako was a hoot. "No, sarge. I don't reckon they have," Henderson said and chuckled. "RPGs have slowed down at least. They're probably saving them for the next choppers or a convoy to show up. I don't know where they got a mortar though."

"I guess they know what they're doing," Bashir said. He coughed and shifted himself around, trying to get comfortable. Or as comfortable as he could in the situation. He had been roughed up a bit by the blast. Mako could tell Bashir would need time to recover.

"They do," Henderson said. "Getting smarter all the time."

"I need to take my man to the bunker," Mako said. "After that, where do you want me?"

"Right here," Henderson said. "One of those RPGs took out our mortar. With this weather, I can't get authorization for artillery from Air Base Thorsness. Once they figure that out, they're probably going to try an attack and overrun us. They know they have us outnumbered. Can you PJs shoot?"

Mako and Bashir looked at each other, trying not to smile. PJs were some of the most highly trained special operators in the US military. They swam, parachuted, ran, or fought their way to injured military personnel wherever they were. They had twenty-eight weeks of combat medical training made that them invaluable contributors in any conflict.

"We can shoot," Mako said.

"All right," Henderson said. "I've got to go check on the forward position. I'm going to send a couple of my guys over here. Take positions along this wall and keep an eye out. My lieutenant is in that bunker." He pointed to a concrete building in the center of the compound. "Says we're only getting intermittent contact with Air Base Thorsness. My guess is they probably can't send any help out in this storm. That bunker is also our fallback position. If we can't hold them off, head there." Henderson got ready to move out.

"One thing, Sergeant," Mako said. "We've lost track of Airman Smith in all the excitement. If you spot him, send him back. Unless you need him. He's our team sniper."

"Will do," Henderson said. He turned and ran, bent over at the waist. He disappeared among the sandbags.

"So," Bashir said. "This is what a Forward Operating Base is like. Nice. Too bad the pool is closed."

"You're a strange dude, Bash," Mako said. "Come on."

Mako got his arm underneath Bashir's shoulders. They struggled their way the few dozen yards to the bunker. Mako got Bashir secured there. Then he stormed back to his position on the northern wall.

Gunfire sounded like popcorn off in the distance. Mako peered over the sandbag. The FOB was right at the entrance to the valley. A small village of huts and shops stood about two hundred yards straight north. Even more places for the bad guys to hide in. There were steep canyon walls on either side of the village. It was high ground, and the terrorists could almost shoot straight down into the compound.

"I'm not a big fan of our position," Mako said. "No offense to our army brothers."

"None taken," a voice behind Mako said. It surprised him, and he nearly jumped. Two of Henderson's men appeared and took cover at the wall.

"I'm Holt, and this is Baker," Holt said. "Welcome to FOB Falcon."

"Chief Master Sergeant Marks," Mako said. "Call me Mako. Everyone does."

"Mako?" Holt said. "I'll bet there's a story behind that."

"Several," Mako said. "So, what do we do, corporal?"

"To be honest, sergeant," Holt said, "We hold this position at all costs. Pretty soon they're going to get tired of hiding behind rocks. They'll come out when they get bored and want a straight-up fight."

"Excellent," Mako said. "What about wounded? Any injuries I can treat?"

Holt shook his head. "There's another PJ on the forward wall treating minor injuries. You guys got Washington out. Luckily, we haven't had many serious injuries yet."

"Wait!" Mako said. "Another PJ? Was his name Smith by any chance?"

"I think so," Holt said. "Our introductions were brief. Because of all the shooting."

"He's okay? Not injured?" Mako asked.

"Didn't seem to be," Holt said. "Kind of a big dude? Blond hair?"

"That's him," Mako said. "It's a good thing he's not injured. Now I can kill him when he gets back."

Holt shrugged. "Looks like we're clear for now."

"Roger that," Mako said. "Let's hope it stays that way."

There was a temporary lull in the shooting. Mako wondered where Smith was. The wind was picking up and the sky was darkening with giant dust clouds.

"Bash, stay frosty," Mako said into his comm. "We've got a poor position and worse visibility. Terrorists could walk right up and pants us right now. We'd never know they were there."

The whistling sound came again. The mortar shell streaked through the sky. It overshot the compound, landing about thirty yards beyond the bunker.

Sergeant Henderson appeared out the gloom with two other soldiers in tow.

"Sergeant Marks, I've got two more—"

Henderson didn't get a chance to finish. A thunderous round of enemy fire came from the village and the canyon walls. RPGs, mortars, and machine gun fire lit up the gloomy sky. Henderson shouting "incoming" was the last thing Mako remembered before the action started.

CHAPTER 5

Location: FOB Falcon, Shashim Valley,
           Kunar Provence, Afghanistan
Date: August 14th
Time: 0741 hours

Senior Airman Phil Smith knew he was in big trouble. When they first fast-roped down from Pedro One, Mako and Bashir went right to work on the Cat Alpha, a patient that had been seriously wounded and needed immediate treatment. Smith made his way through the compound, treating assorted smaller injuries. Right now, he worked on a young soldier who had been shot in the hip. He had to work quickly.

"Hold this here," Smith said. He took the soldier's hand and placed it over the clotting bandage.

"That's it," Smith said. "You're doing fine."

Smith administered pain medication and a dose of antibiotics to combat infection. He checked the soldier's blood pressure. It was stable.

"What's your name, soldier?" Smith asked.

"Mayfair," the soldier said through gritted teeth.

"Where are you from?" Smith asked.

"West Virginia," Mayfair said.

Another soldier leaned against the wall next to Mayfair. His arm was burned. Smith rinsed it off with some bottled water. Next, he applied an antibiotic ointment. Then pain medication.

A sergeant appeared out the gloom and huddled next to Smith. His name tag said Henderson.

"Are you Airman Smith?" he asked.

"Yes," Smith said.

"I've got a message from your chief," Henderson said.

"I'll bet," Smith said.

"He wants you to return to his position," Henderson said.

"I'm sure," Smith said.

Henderson laughed. "Is he always so . . . big?"

"Yeah," Smith said. "That's Mako."

"He says you're a sniper?" Henderson asked.

"I've graduated from the school," Smith said.

"Feel like using those skills?" Henderson asked.

Smith glanced around the compound. There was a lull in the fighting.

"It doesn't seem like a target-rich environment," Smith said.

"Maybe not, but your sergeant said I could use you if necessary," Henderson said. "This will keep you from taking a bunch of grief from your chief."

"I'm listening," Smith said.

Henderson drew some shapes in the dirt. "We're here," he said, making an X in the dirt. "The village is over here. They've got the mortar set up here," Henderson said. "We've got to take it out, or they'll pick us off one at a time. I want to send some men over to take out that mortar. I'll put you here, and you can provide overwatch for them."

"Sergeant," Smith said. "I'll do whatever you need me to do. But I can't shoot what I can't see with the storm."

"You'll be fine," Henderson said. "Don't worry. I got a plan." He smiled at Smith.

As bullets pinged overhead, Smith could only smile back.

⊚ CHAPTER 6

The gunfire sounded far off. Mako could not open
his eyes. He felt sick to is stomach. His head pounded.
It was eerily quiet. He needed to get to his feet. The
Taliban could attack at any time.

He tried to sit up. The world spun away from him.
"Ugh," he groaned. "Bash? Bash are you—" He
thought it was strange he couldn't see Bashir. Then he
remembered. Bashir was in the bunker with the other
wounded. He tried to sit up again. This time he managed
to get one arm under him. Throwing his shoulders
against the wall, he finally managed to find his balance.

Mako rubbed his head. His fingers came away
bloody. He pulled a gauze pad from his medkit and
wiped the blood from his eyes. It wasn't a serious wound.
Mako did a self-assessment. His right ankle was hurting.
But he was in decent shape. No gunshot wounds or other
serious injuries. Although the way his head hurt, he
might have a concussion.

His last memory was of hunkering down behind the sandbags with Sergant Henderson. Then came the vicious counterattack. And now? He didn't see the sergeant. What was his name? Henderson. What happened to him?

Mako's vision cleared. His head stopped spinning. Over the sound of the gunfire, he heard a groan. Glancing around, he spotted a boot sticking out from underneath debris.

"Henderson!" Mako shouted. He scrambled across the ground to the downed airman's side. He moved rocks and dirt until he could see his face.

The young sergeant's face was chalky white, and he wasn't breathing.

Mako wasted no time. He quickly checked Henderson's neck for fractures. Finding none, he turned his head to the side, clearing the airway. Henderson coughed up a bunch of phlegm and dust. He was breathing at least.

With his stethoscope him his kit, Mako listened to Henderson's lungs. One of them crackled and wheezed. Henderson might have had a puncture. He groaned and tried to sit up.

"Whoa! Whoa!" Mako said. He pushed Henderson

gently back to the ground and said, "You ain't goin' anywhere."

"Where are we?" Henderson moaned.

"We are on an all-expenses paid trip to beautiful Afghanistan," Mako said. "Courtesy of your Uncle Sam. Now, your work is done for the day. You've probably got a concussion and a punctured lung. Your leg doesn't look so hot. But today is your lucky day, Sergeant Henderson."

Henderson groaned. "Why is it my lucky day, sarge?"

"It is your lucky day, sergeant," Mako said, "because you have good fortune. You're being treated by the greatest PJ in the entire history of US Air Force Pararescue. There is no rougher, tougher special operator in the entire US military. And it is your good fortune, sergeant, that he is here to devote his full attention to you."

"Great," Henderson said. "That's just great."

"OK," Mako said. "I've got to move you. Don't want you lying down with that lung. This is gonna hurt."

"I'm ready," Henderson said.

Mako grasped Henderson underneath the arms.

He pulled him up until he could sit and lean against the sandbag wall. Henderson nearly passed out. Mako gave him painkillers. In a few minutes he was relaxed.

"Get me patched up, please, sarge," Henderson said. "From the sounds of it, there's a lot of shooting going on."

"Your shooting days are done for now, sergeant," Mako said.

"Negative, sarge!" Henderson said. "Somebody has to coordinate our defenses!"

"And that someone ain't you," Mako said. "Not today. I appreciate the desire, son. But you are in no shape to be partaking in any Army type activity. That includes shooting, tossing grenades, or other such duties as assigned."

"Sarge—"

Henderson didn't get any further.

"It's been decided, sergeant," Mako said. "No need to keep discussin' it."

The firefight raged back and forth. Mako tried his radio. No luck. It couldn't reach Air Base Thorsness. It couldn't pick up any signal at all. Mako removed Henderson's radio from its clip. He clicked the microphone on and off. No signal.

"All right," Mako said. "You're stable. You stay here. Anybody comes by, you see if they have a working radio. I'm—"

Mako's word were cut off by a loud explosion. In the sky above them, rocket fire struck a helicopter. It careened across the sky and crashed into the eastern side of the canyon.

Mako watched from behind the sandbags.

When the chopper went down, he unleashed a string of curses. "Pedro Two! Pedro Two! Come in, over!" he shouted into his radio. All he heard was static. "Stupid radio!" he shouted in frustration.

Mako needed to think. They needed to get a team to that chopper as soon as possible. The Taliban forces would overrun the site. If there were injured, they'd be in grave danger of being captured or killed.

"I'm going to hustle up volunteers and head for that wounded bird," Mako said. "When you get a minute, reboot your comm system. See if the radio will come back up. If it does, call AB Thorsness and get reinforcements, artillery, anything."

"Roger that," Henderson said.

Mako rose up and sprinted toward the northern position. Gunfire and explosions echoed around him. For the life of him, he couldn't understand why someone would choose the ground to fight on. It would be one thing if you were ambushed trying to cross it. Quite another if you made a conscious decision to fight here.

The chaos thickened. He wondered if the insurgents would ever run out of ammunition. The air was darkened with sand and grit. The second Pave Hawk hovered above the crash site. Its guns were blazing as it did everything it could to keep the enemy from overrunning the site. But it couldn't hold that positon forever. Mako knew they would run out of ammunition. And with the weather, they could be forced to land.

"Got to give it to that pilot," Mako said to himself. "He's just begging to be shot down." Mako continued his run. Bullets stung the ground near him, which made every step dangerous.

"Smith!" Mako shouted as he maneuvered through the compound. He made sure to keep his head down. "Airman Smith!" Mako hoped the young PJ was not among the wounded.

"Hey, PJ!" a voice from behind Mako shouted. "Get down!" Something crashed into the back of his legs. Mako tumbled backwards. A mortar round exploded thirty yards away. He lay on the ground too stunned to move. He thought his eardrums might have burst, but slowly the ringing sound subsided. He groaned and scrambled to his hands and knees.

"Who goes there?" Mako said.

A soldier in body armor untangled himself from Mako's legs and rose to his knees.

"I don't think so!" Mako said in surprise. "No way somebody as scrawny as you took down Chief Master Sergeant Marks."

"You're welcome," the soldier said.

"What's your name, soldier?" Mako said.

"Private First Class Jason Sparks, Sergeant, sir," Sparks said.

"Private Sparks," Mako said. "As of this minute, you are hereby a member of the 223rd Pararescue battalion of the United States Air Force. Any questions?"

Sparks was lean and wiry. He was maybe 5 feet 8 inches tall. His helmet threatened to swallow his head.

"I . . . sergeant," Sparks stammered. "I don't want to get in trouble for abandoning my post."

"You won't," Mako said. "I'll square it with your

CO. In fact, I'll call the Secretary of the Army if necessary. But I've got important business. I need you to help me find your lieutenant, who is out here somewhere. Provided he hasn't been wounded."

"Okay, sergeant," Sparks said. "I guess it's all right then. What are your orders?"

"It's simple," Mako said, hefting his rifle. "We're going up there to get our people. These things we do, Private Sparks."

"Hooah," Sparks said.

⊚ CHAPTER 7

Location: FOB Falcon, Shashim Valley,
Afghanistan, Pave Hawk Pedro One
crash site
Date: August 14th
Time: 0715 hours

Malik could not believe his luck. He had been in
many firefights—but never an attack this large and
coordinated. When the shooting commenced, the
noise echoed off the walls of the canyon, amplifying
the sound. The volume was immediate and intense.
The noise was gone one minute and there the next, as
if the hills would never be quiet again.

"Reload!" a man operating an RPG shouted. The
yell shook him out of his daze. Malik bent to the task.
Removing another rocket from the crate, he shoved
it home in the launcher. He bent away, covering his
ear as the man fired. "Whoosh!" The RPG left the
launcher and streaked across the sky like lightning.
Down below them, the American soldiers were taking
a horrible beating.

For the first few minutes, his task was easy. Reload
and then reload again. A sound he didn't recognize

churned up the hill, followed by the metallic zing of bullets. The soldiers below had recovered and were returning fire.

"Cover!" the man with the RPG shouted. Malik clutched his rifle and crouched behind a nearby boulder. Bullets ripped up the dirt where he'd stood not a second before.

The sun was coming up. He did not think the Americans could see him in the low morning light. They were firing at muzzle flashes. It was still cool in the valley. But Malik's face was drenched in sweat. The Americans were putting up a good fight, but he did not know how long they would last. He had heard talk that morning of the storm coming that would keep their planes and helicopters grounded. They considered it a sign that God was on their side. To Malik, watching the bullets fly all around from everywhere, it appeared that God had chosen no one.

A new sound cut through the noise of small arms fire. Malik risked a peek over the boulder, and to the west he spotted two American helicopters. How could this be? Perhaps the storm was not so bad yet to keep them from flying.

He and his fellow fighters hated American aircraft. They were capable of unleashing so much fire and destruction. It made it hard to keep fighters disciplined. They could not be in a prolonged fight with Americans when they could bring their air muscle to bear. Even the most dedicated soldier of Allah found it nearly impossible to stand before an A-10 or a Pave Hawk raining down death upon them.

It was why the Taliban had developed quick-strike tactics like these. They used surprise and the terrain to their advantage. Then they melted away before airpower could arrive.

The helicopters drew closer. The insurgents turned their attention toward the incoming craft. Machine gun rounds and RPGs whizzed through the sky. Even at this distance, Malik could hear the bullets pinging off the metal armor of the Pave Hawks.

At first, he thought his eyes were deceiving him. From the corner of his vision, he saw an RPG burst through the sky and collide with the lead Pave Hawk. There was a loud explosion. The helicopter jerked as if a giant had plucked it from the sky. A large plume of smoke coiled out of the engine. The rotors made a high-pitched sound.

The chopper twisted and bucked in the sky. The pilot fought for control. It was losing altitude. It jerked to the left and then back to the right. It was closer now. When one of the engines finally exploded, the chopper spun around in a circle. It was going to crash.

And Malik would be very lucky if it didn't land right on top of him.

◎ CHAPTER 8

Location: FOB Falcon, Shashim Valley,
          Afghanistan, Pave Hawk Pedro One
          crash site
Date: August 14th
Time: 0907 hours

Lieutenant Jamal Jenkins couldn't remember feeling like this. His shoulders had somehow caught fire. His eyes stung, and he smelled smoke. When he tried to move, he instantly regretted it.

Jenkins didn't know it at the time, but he had a severe concussion. Thinking of any kind was painful. Still, his training took over. He couldn't see. Something wet was running in his eyes. When he tried to raise an arm to clear his eyes, his shoulder and his concussed brain objected. The pain in his shoulder was intense and burning. He wanted to cry out but he worried it would make his head hurt.

First steps. Breathing. He was breathing. Carefully, he took a deep breath in and let it out slowly. Once more. And again. It did little to stop the pain, but it was now easier to think.

Bleeding. He needed to know if he was losing blood.

Yet he couldn't move. What about the other shoulder? The one that didn't feel like it had been ripped from his body. It was his left arm. He moved it a little. No pain. But now it was stuck.

Keep breathing, Jenkins told himself. In and out. He found that with each breath his mind cleared a tiny bit.

Jenkins' arm was twisted around him. He was lying on it. Opening his eyes, all he saw was a ground-level view of the dirt. There were rocks and pieces of shrapnel scattered everywhere. He tried to lift his head up for a better view. Pushing beneath him with his good arm, he finally rolled over onto his back. He tried to contain it, but an agonizing groan escaped his lips.

"Whoo," Jenkins gasped. He'd been thrown from the wreckage. Now he tried taking inventory of his injuries. His brain felt like it was encased in mud. Possible concussion. His left shoulder was burning. He couldn't tell if it was broken or dislocated. He had cuts and abrasions on his face.

"Loot!" a voice said from the wreckage. "Loot! Are you there?"

"Hey!" Jenkins said. "Hey, over here."

Sergeant George appeared out of the thickening dust.

"Loot!" he said as he dropped to his knees beside Jenkins. George immediately went to work examining his CRO. Jenkins tried to stop him.

"No, George, stop," Jenkins said. "What about Garcia? The aircrew?"

"You're the first person I've come across, Loot," George said.

"Okay," Jenkins said. "Help me up. We've got to look for them."

"Lieutenant," George said. "You're in no shape to be looking for anyone."

"Sergeant," Jenkins said. He tried to sit up, but he was overcome by dizziness. "Whoa," he said and slumped back down.

"Let me treat you, lieutenant," George said. "Then we'll figure out what to do."

Jenkins groaned and tried to sit up again. Then he stopped.

"Sergeant George," Jenkins said. "I think we've got bigger problems."

"What's that, lieutenant?" George asked.

"Those guys over there," Jenkins said. "I think they're the Taliban."

"What next, sergeant?" Sparks asked.

"Can you get a couple of volunteers?" Mako watched as the soldiers scurried around the compound. They were firing their weapons and putting up a defense against the attack. It was controlled chaos.

"I reckon I could," Sparks said. "Can I ask what you want them to volunteer for?"

"Sure," Mako said. "We're going to hustle up to that crash site and see if any of our people are injured. Nothing to it."

"Um, sergeant," Sparks said quietly. "No disrespect intended. Maybe they do things different in the Air Force. In infantry school they taught us not to cross open ground and willingly expose ourselves to the enemy fire."

"The Air Force has the same rules," Mako said. "But rules go out the window in combat. My team might even be on that Pave Hawk. They could be injured. Maybe even dead. And worst of all, that bird crashed a lot closer to the bad guys than it did us. So, I'm going up there to get them. The only question I have is, am I going alone?"

"No, sergeant," Sparks said. "Not alone. I'll get some guys together. With Sergeant Henderson down, I don't know who is in charge here. It might even be you. Let's make our way to the north position. That's the side closest to the crash."

Bent at the waist, Mako and Sparks hugged the sandbag wall as they trotted across the compound. They passed a machine gun nest. The gunner and his loader kept up a furious fire on the enemy position. Midway through the compound, Mako spotted a familiar sight. Several injured soldiers were laid out. They were being tended to by Smith.

"Smith," Mako said. "If you aren't a sight for sore eyes. Where have you been?"

"Hey, sarge!" Smith said. "After we roped in, I started treating the injured. Once I got one treated, another popped up. Their Lieutenant is down with a GSW. He went down early in the fight. I lost track of their sergeant. I think he was keeping things under control.

I'm out of plasma and almost no painkillers left."

Mako shrugged off his pack, which was full of medical gear.

"Here," Mako said. "Take some of my supplies. Not everything though, because Sparks and I are going on a mission."

"A mission?" Smith asked. He took some of Mako's bandages, a couple of IV bags, and some painkillers.

"We need to get to that chopper," Mako said. "Before the Taliban does."

"Sarge," Smith said. "Forgive me, but that's nuts. You should wait until reinforcements get here. We've got all we can handle right here."

"No time to wait, airman," Mako said. "You stay here, tend to the wounded. Sparks, you round up two more men."

They left Smith with the wounded. Sparks and Mako finally reached the northern wall. There were six soldiers there. Two of them were using a .30 caliber machine gun.

Sparks was next to him, with two fresh-faced soldiers. "Sergeant," Sparks said. "This is Collins and Mullins. They volunteered to go."

"All right, that's the spirit," Mako said. "Let's get

extra ammo, water, and grenades. Sparks, you find someone here who can call for an air strike the instant the conditions improve. Sparks, give that machine gunner the sign we're going over. We're going to count on them to give us covering fire."

When everything was set, they gathered at the northern wall. The .30 caliber fired.

"Go! Go! Go!" Mako said. The four of them scrambled over the wall. Mako was glad the sky was full of blowing sand. It gave them some cover.

Mako took point and headed toward the chopper. It didn't take long for enemy fire to find them. Bullets whizzed through the air and chopped up the dirt at their feet.

"Nothing to it, boys!" Mako shouted. "Let's go!"

Sparks looked at Collins and Mullins and shrugged.

"I guess they make them crazy in the Air Force," Sparks said.

◎ CHAPTER 10

Location: FOB Falcon, Shashim Valley,
         Afghanistan
Date: August 14th
Time: 0743 hours

Malik coughed and spat as sand filled his nose and mouth. When the chopper hit the ground with a loud boom, it kicked up a huge cloud of dust. The aircraft shrieked and moaned as it plowed through the dirt. Pieces of the fuselage broke off and spun across the ground like shrapnel.

It came to a rest about forty yards from Malik's position. Some of the larger pieces were on fire. A loud cheer went up from the fighters stationed in the rocks nearby. Shooting down an American helicopter required a celebration.

"Come," the man with an RPG said. He slung the rocket launcher over his shoulder. His rifle was an AK-47, just like Malik's. They left their spot behind the boulder and crept toward the wreckage. There was another Pave Hawk hovering above them.

"What about the helicopter?" Malik asked.

"They will not shoot anymore," the man said. "They fear hitting one of the crew. There may be survivors in the wreckage."

Malik could not imagine how anyone could survive such a crash. Even if they somehow lived through the impact, the fire and smoke would likely kill them.

Malik followed the man as they picked their way down the canyon. It took a few hours to get to the helicopter. There were no sounds coming from it. He saw no movement among the wreckage.

"What is our plan?" Malik asked, feeling he had a right to know.

"We will look for any equipment that can be salvaged," the man said. "Weapons, supplies, anything that survived the crash."

Malik couldn't help but feel nervous. It felt like the helicopter was still dangerous. Even after it was shot down and broken apart. He wondered if the Americans built their planes and helicopters to look scary on purpose. It worked. The scattered and broken pieces of the Pave Hawk still felt threatening.

The largest piece of the downed chopper was only twenty yards away now.

Malik jumped when the man with the RPG cried out. A red flower appeared on his chest, and he crumpled to the ground. He was dead. Bullets pinged into the ground and off the nearby rocks. Malik was taking fire.

He was wrong. Someone had survived the crash. And they were shooting at him.

CHAPTER 11

Location: FOB Falcon, Shashim Valley
Afghanistan
Date: August 14th
Time: 0958 hours

"Fire! Fire!" Jenkins shouted.

Sergeant George spun and let off a burst from his M-4. The whole situation was going sideways. The Taliban fighters were advancing on the crash site. They would try to scavenge anything of use. As far as he knew, the Taliban did not usually take prisoners. Jenkins determined they would not go down without a fight.

A fighter carrying an RPG tumbled to the ground. He was with a younger man who carried an AK-47. George fired in his direction and missed. But the shots drove him into cover.

"We need to move, Loot," George said. "We're too exposed here."

"Roger," Lieutenant Jenkins said. "There's a large section of fuselage over there. We can get behind it."

"Hang on," George said. He grabbed Jenkins by the collar of his armored vest. George was a strong man.

But he was winded, and Jenkins and his equipment probably totaled over 200 pounds.

He jerked on the collar and dragged him over the ground. Jenkins let out a yell. George winced. "Sorry, Loot!" George said. "I can give you some fetanyl."

"Negative," Jenkins said. "I need to keep a clear head."

"Roger that," George said.

Their cover was about ten yards today. With a last surge of energy, George pulled the lieutenant behind the wreckage.

"Keep alert," Jenkins said. "I don't suppose your radio is working, is it?"

"No, sir," George said. He slapped a new clip of ammo into the M-4.

George glanced around the wreckage. What he wouldn't give for a battalion of marines right about now. Bullets whizzed through the air.

George pulled the lieutenant behind it with one last lunge.

"You okay, Loot?" George asked.

Jenkins groaned.

"Yeah. Keep your eyes moving, sergeant. We're like fish in a barrel down here."

As if to confirm his thought, the enemy sent another hail of gunfire at their position. George watched as three Taliban fighters emerged from the brush. He fired a burst from his M-4, but it didn't slow them down. Then the Pave Hawk still overhead got into the fight. The .50 caliber machine gun took care of the immediate threat.

The relief was momentary.

"I've got six more fighters coming in," George said. He readied his M-4, sighting over the top of the wreckage.

"Do you have any grenades?" Jenkins asked.

"No, sir," George said. "Fresh out."

"Sure would be handy if we had some grenades," Jenkins said.

"No doubt," George said.

George kept firing his M-4. "It's my last clip, Loot," George said. In a few seconds the clip ejected from his rifle.

The Taliban fighters were surrounding them now. George pulled his pistol from the holster.

"If we go down," George said. "We're going down fighting."

"Hooah, sergeant," Jenkins said.

From the gunfire, it felt like the enemy was right on top of them. All that George could do was raise his pistol and fire blindly over the wreckage. Then he heard a clattering sound, and something bounced into the dirt beside them.

"Grenade!" Jenkins shouted. There was no time to move or cover.

The last thing George remembered was feeling like someone had punched him in the stomach with a sledgehammer.

⊙ CHAPTER 12

Garcia awoke to a terrifying sight. Mako was bending over him, staring into his face.

"Garcia," Mako said, shaking his shoulder. "Garcia, you hurt?"

"Yes," Garcia moaned. "I am now. Don't sneak up on a guy like that, Mako."

"Where?" Mako said. "Where does it hurt, Garcia? Talk to me."

"Is my entire body a place?" Garcia asked.

"Very funny, sergeant," Mako said. "You gave me a big scare."

"I gave you a scare?" Garcia said. "I was in a helicopter crash."

"Yeah, some guys will do anything for attention," Mako said. "Seriously. Any injuries?"

Garcia flexed his wrist. "My wrist hurts," he said. "Oh, and my head. My head is definitely injured."

Mako checked Garcia's eyes with a penlight.

"Maybe a mild concussion," Mako said.

Mako helped Garcia to his feet. The air around them was now full of sand, the wind howling through the mouth of the canyon. The only saving grace was that they hadn't lost their equipment.

"Did you check on the aircrew?" Garcia asked.

"We did," Mako said. "But the cabin was empty."

Garcia was alarmed. "Did you find George and the lieutenant?" Garcia asked. He feared the worst.

"No," Mako said. "There was no sign of them. They were on board with you?"

"Yeah," Garcia said. "I wonder . . ."

"Hey, sarge, over here," Sparks said. He was standing by a large chunk of wreckage.

"Garcia," Mako said. "This is Private First Class Sparks. By the authority vested in me, I have promoted him to the PJs. These other two are Mullins and Collins. They're PJs now too."

"There's a lot of tracks around here," Sparks said, pointing to the ground. "Whoever walked off that way was carrying something heavy."

"You think—" Mako said.

"Makes sense," Sparks said. "Look. When a

chopper crashes there are two outcomes. Survivors, sometimes with injuries, or fatalities. Since we don't have bodies, either somebody carried out the bodies, or they've been taken prisoner. If they were taken prisoner, they went that way."

"Garcia," Mako said. "Are you up to a hike?"

Garcia nodded.

"All right," Mako said. "Let's saddle up."

◉ CHAPTER 13

Location: FOB Falcon, Shashim Valley,
            Afghanistan
Date: August 14th
Time: 1017 hours

Malik was astonished by how quickly things changed in combat.

It all started with a surprise attack on an American base. The battle had been fought to a draw. Malik assumed they would withdraw, melting away into the countryside. This is how they had been fighting for years, with short, planned attacks. They tried to inflict as much damage on the enemy as possible. Afterwards, they'd fade into the countryside.

Regroup and repeat.

But then a helicopter was shot down. It was a great victory to shoot down an American aircraft. The Taliban could not compete with American airpower. To knock one out of the skies was a tremendous morale booster, even if it came from a lucky shot.

Once an aircraft was shot down, it was a race to the crash site. They would take anything of value.

Equipment, ammunition, and if they were able, prisoners. It was rare for any crew to survive a crash.

That is what surprised Malik. As they raced to the crash site, someone popped up from the wreckage. Their return fire sent Malik and the other fighters scrambling for cover. The man who fired the RPG was killed. Another fighter picked up the RPG launcher.

Nothing was ever left behind.

Malik was huddled behind a small boulder. He felt more in danger than he was when they were attacking the base. The enemy was closer. And if they were injured, they would be more desperate.

Malik peered around the rock. He saw the head of an American behind the wreckage. It ducked away. There were three other fighters to his left, and four to his right. The American must know that he was surrounded. They moved closer. He could not have much more ammunition.

One of the fighters to the left rushed the wreckage. Malik heard the crack of a pistol, and the man spun into the ground, dead. Another pistol shot, and one of the men to his right screamed and clutched his arm.

The wind whipped up and gave them a chance to surround the wreckage. To Malik's surprise, there were two Americans huddled there. An injured man was on the ground. The other American covered the injured one with own body.

Three more fighters appeared, leading the two pilots at gunpoint. The Americans shouted at them, but no one among them spoke English. The gunfire in the valley had died down. The rest of their force was likely withdrawing.

The injured American could not walk. Two men grabbed him by the arms and legs and carried him east toward the canyon. The other Americans were tied up and ordered to march. Malik and his men would take them to their network of caves about ten kilometers from the canyon.

Malik wondered if they were doing the right thing. The Americans were crazed about recovering their dead and wounded. They would send more aircraft and ground troops to get their comrades back. Holding these men captive would send the full might of the American military down upon them.

It did not matter. Malik was young. It was not his place to make these decisions. All he could do was fight. If more troops came after them, he would do his duty.

The air was thick and dark. It was approaching midmorning. The sky was full of blowing sand. It looked like someone had hung a curtain over them. Sand and pebbles whipped at their faces and eyes.

Malik tried not to study the American captives. They moved across the valley, going around the village. In a short while they were in the foothills of the canyon. Malik wondered how many fighters had survived this encounter with the Americans. What happened to Abdul? Despite his tendency to talk too much, he was a friend.

They kept up a good pace. Each of them took turns helping to carry the wounded American. Malik looked back the way they had come.

He could not help but feel that danger was close on their trail.

◉ CHAPTER 14

Location: East of FOB Falcon,
         Shashim Valley, Kunar Provence,
         Afghanistan
Date: August 14th
Time: 1104 hours

"Are you sure, Sparks?" Mako asked. "You haven't lost the trail?"

"I'm sure, sergeant," Sparks said. "About ten people in the group. Somebody carrying something heavy. Headed north."

"I hope it isn't goat farmers on their way home from the village," Mako said.

"I don't think so," Sparks said. "They're in a hurry, not trying to hide. They must not think anyone will be coming after them."

"Well they couldn't be more wrong," Mako said.

"Sergeant," Sparks said. "Are you sure you don't want to wait for reinforcements?"

"We could," Mako said. "But if they've got our guys, any extra time wasted and they can move them deep in the country. We'd never find them. Better to keep up the heat."

The five men moved quickly through the countryside. They were spread out in a roughly diamond shape formation about ten to fifteen yards between them. Collins took point. Mako was pretty sure they'd been spotted by lookouts. That was fine with Mako. He wanted them to know they were coming without delay.

"The best thing," Mako had said. "Would be for them to turn over our guys right now. Don't see that happening though."

Sparks kept following the tracks. Before long, it was clear they moved onto a well-traveled trail.

Sparks put his arm up. His fist was clenched at a right angle to his body. Everyone stopped. Sparks waved Mako forward.

"What is it, private?" Mako asked.

"What I was afraid of, sergeant," Sparks said. He pointed to the ground a few feet in front of them. A thin line of black string crossed the path.

"Booby trap," Sparks said. "Don't see where it leads. But they come up on the compound and steal our claymores all the time. I think we need to go around."

"Roger that," Mako said. Sparks took a strip of cloth from his pocket and marked the spot. Someone

would come back and deal with it later.

Sparks waved everyone around. They came back together as the trail narrowed at the mouth of a dry streambed.

"Pretty good spot for an ambush," Sparks said.

The words were hardly out of his mouth before the ground around them exploded in gunfire.

◉ CHAPTER 15

Location: Shashim Valley,
          Kunar Province, Afghanistan
Date: August 14th
Time: 1121 hours

Their plan had worked to perfection.

Malik was glad. They had left a booby trap across the trail one kilometer back. They deliberately made it easy to find. Once it was discovered, the team following them would likely move toward the canyon wall, where the ground was rockier and booby traps were easier to spot. That would lead them to the mouth of the dry streambed. There Malik and the others would be waiting for them.

With the air full of sand and the wind blowing, visibility was down to about thirty yards. The Americans emerged from the gloom. It felt to Malik as if they were close enough to touch. When all five of them came into sight, they opened fire. One of the soldiers was immediately hit in the shoulder. The others dove for cover. The Americans shot back. The fight was on.

Malik was in a stand of trees with two other fighters.

They were the closest to the Americans. They had been told to try and flank them. Malik rose up to fire his AK-47. An explosion to his right sent him tumbling to the ground. His left leg felt like it was on fire. He looked down to see a large chunk of his calf had been torn away. He groaned in agony. The other two fighters were down. Another explosion rocked the ground and sent dirt and rocks tumbling through the air. Stones pelted his head and shoulders.

The Americans had grenades. Not only that, they were moving rapidly forward, not concerned about cover. They were determined to retrieve their comrades.

Malik emptied his rifle in their direction. He wasn't sure he hit anything. The Americans would be on top of him if he didn't move. Raising himself up, he tried to stand on one leg, but the pain was too great. He fell to the ground. When he rolled over, he was looking up at the face of a very large American, who pointed a rifle right at his head.

Malik raised his hands.

◎ CHAPTER 16

"Incoming!" Sparks said. "Cover! Cover! Cover!"

Gunshots rang out of the gloom ahead. The Taliban had been waiting for them to reach the streambed. They were ready. Mullins was struck in the shoulder but his body armor took the brunt of it.

Collins and Garcia popped up. They returned fire, forcing the Taliban to retreat. While they did, Mako, Sparks, and Mullins ran forward.

"Suppressing fire!" Mako said. This time, Garcia and Collins ran forward. Mako, Sparks, and Mullins provided the covering fire. Each time, they moved closer to the Taliban positions.

Mullins launched two grenades from his M-240. The explosions were deafening.

"We got someone," Garcia said. "I could hear them shout."

"I hear movement, sarge," Sparks said.

"OK," Mako said. "Let's go. Watch out for the wounded. They're still armed."

Mako led the group into the trees. There were two dead Taliban fighters on his right. Up ahead, he could see the undergrowth moving. Like someone was trying to crawl away.

"Garcia!" Mako whispered. He pointed to the grass. Garcia nodded, raising his weapon.

"Hold it!" Mako said. A Taliban fighter was crawling along the ground. His leg was wounded.

The man rolled over, his hands raised in surrender.

"Good grief," Mako said. "It's just a kid."

"He's injured," Garcia said. He took the boy's rifle and handed it to Collins. Without the gun, the boy looked even smaller.

"They send kids in to do the fighting?" Mako asked. His faced soured. He looked like he wanted to squash something.

Sparks shrugged. "Yeah, well. Unfortunately, it's not that unusual. I've seen a lot of kids on the battlefield even younger."

"What kind of world do we live in?" Mako said. "Big enough to carry a gun, big enough to answer questions. Any of you three speak Farsi?"

"Collins." Sparks gestured and Collins stepped forward.

"Collins knows some of the local dialects," Sparks said.

"Ask him where they're keeping the prisoners," Mako said.

Collins spoke to the boy.

"He claims he doesn't know," Collins said.

Collins interrogated the boy again. He still refused to talk.

"Garcia," Mako said. "Let's take a look at his leg." He removed the medkit from his ruck.

The boy's eyes grew wide and his hands shook. Garcia irrigated the wound. He finished it off with a pressure bandage. The boy looked surprised and confused, as if he couldn't understand why they were treating him well. With the pain killers administered, the boy realized he could stand up. Before they could stop him, he got up and limped beside a tree.

Mako stood up as well. He loaded a new clip into his M-4 and racked the slide.

"All right," Mako said. "We're running out of time. Tell the kid he's got fifteen seconds to tell us what we want to know."

"Mako?" Garcia said.

Mako didn't reply, he just stared at the kid. He reached into his pack and removed a chocolate protein bar. He unwrapped it and walked over next to the boy. He handed the bar to their prisoner.

The boy looked at the bar and licked his lips.

"He's hungry," Mako said. "Probably hasn't had much to eat in days."

The boy still wouldn't take the bar. Mako broke it in half and held out a piece. The boy could not hold back. He grabbed the chocolate from Mako's hand and wolfed it down.

Mako held out the other piece. The boy disposed of that one as well.

"Ask him again, Collins," Mako said.

This time the boy told them everything they wanted to know.

◉ CHAPTER 17

Location: Shashim Valley, Kunar
            Province, Afghanistan
Date: August 14th
Time: 1051 hours

Lieutenant Jamal Jenkins was trying to stay awake. His eyes wanted to close. Sergeant George quietly begged him to stay awake. The Taliban fighters brought them to a small farmhouse.

"Stay with me, Loot," George said.

"Trying," Jenkins said. "But I'm awfully tired, sergeant."

"I know you are, sir," George said. "But you've got a concussion. I don't have anything to treat you with. So I need you to stay awake."

"Any idea where we are?" Jenkins asked.

"No, sir," George said. "Not exactly. We're somewhere east of FOB Falcon. In the foothills."

"What do you think they plan to do with us?" Jenkins asked.

George was about to answer when they heard gunshots coming from some distance behind them.

The gunfire went back and forth. Then there was a series of explosions.

"That sounded like grenades going off," George said.

"And who are they shooting at?" Jenkins said. "I don't think a rescue party could be sent this quickly."

"Maybe not," George said. "But we crashed near the compound. I wonder if they sent a squad after us."

"I doubt it," Jenkins said.

The Taliban fighters sounded agitated about something. They were arguing in the next room, their voices trampling one over the other.

"What do you suppose is going on?" Jenkins asked.

George didn't get a chance to answer. The windows in the farm house shattered and smoke filled the air. Someone had launched smokers into the building. The fighters ran to the windows, firing their weapons.

George saw his chance.

"Loot? Can you walk on that bum leg if I help you?" George asked.

"I think so," Jenkins said.

"Come on," George said. He put Jenkins' arm over his shoulders and made for the back door. The fighters in the house were distracted. It was slow going.

George threw open the door and hobbled through. Jenkins could barely walk due to his injuries. He grabbed the lieutenant and pulled his torso onto his shoulders in a fireman's carry.

Out the back door, George hustled toward the nearest underbrush.

"We are never going to speak of this again," Jenkins said. He grunted as he was jostled over the rough terrain.

"My lips are sealed," George said. He was grunting with the effort.

They made it to the underbrush. George had to move cautiously now. There could be other Taliban fighters around. The sandstorm still obscured the sun. But he thought he was headed south. Back toward the compound.

They had gone about fifty yards when they heard someone cock a weapon behind them.

"Hands up," a voice said. A voice they both recognized. George helped Jenkins to the ground, and they turned around. There stood Mako, with a big grin on his face.

"They let you have a gun," Jenkins said.

"Didn't leave them with much choice," Mako said.

"Mako, I don't think I've ever been so glad to see that ugly face," Jenkins said.

"What do you say we get out of here?" Mako said.

"Hooah," Jenkins and George answered.

◎ EPILOGUE

Mako gave a thumbs up and the Pave Hawk lowered the pallet of supplies. Food, water, and medicine were tightly packed on the loader. When it reached the ground, Sergeant George unhooked the cable, and the Pave Hawk zoomed away. Villagers crowded around while soldiers from the base handed out water and blankets.

"How much more stuff are they bringing in?" George asked.

"At least two more loads," Mako said.

"We're winning hearts and minds," George said.

"I guess," Mako said. "I'm pretty sure some of them were shooting at us last week."

George laughed. "No doubt," he said.

They went to work helping distribute supplies. In a short time, everything was gone.

"You see him?" George said quietly.

"Yep. Near the coffee shop at two o'clock," Mako said.

A young boy sat in the courtyard of the village near a small shop. He studied the PJs intently. Both George and Mako thought he looked like the young man they'd encountered in the firefight the week before.

"You think that's him?" George asked.

"Pretty sure," Mako said.

When they had returned from freeing Garcia and Jenkins in the caves, the boy was gone. There was a blood trail. Mako considered following after him. But given they were behind enemy lines, he had thought better of it. He had to focus on his teammates first.

Everyone was recovering from their injuries. Lieutenant Jenkins had a pretty serious concussion and a sprained knee. Garcia and George had minor injuries and were healing nicely. Mako refused to acknowledge he had any injuries at all.

The team was assigned to Air Base Thorsness while Jenkins was hospitalized.

"Are we getting a new CRO?" George asked.

"I bet," Mako said.

"Probably somebody green," George groused. "We'll have to spend all our time training him."

"That's how it usually works," Mako said laughing.

Mako glanced over at the shop. The boy was gone.

"Ready?" Mako said to George.

"Always," George said.

They grabbed their rifles and headed back to FOB Falcon. They would be ready for whatever came next. They were PJs.

These things they did so others might live.

CAN'T GET ENOUGH OF PARARESCUE CORPS?
CHECK OUT THE FIRST CHAPTER OF
NILE CHAOS

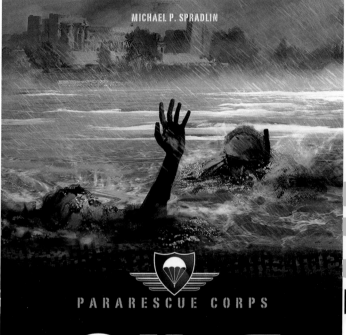

MICHAEL P. SPRADLIN

PARARESCUE CORPS

NILE CHAOS

◎ CHAPTER 1

Location: Kandahar Province, Afghanistan
Date: June 1st
Time: 0600 hours

"Blood pressure is dropping!" Sergeant Garcia shouted over the noise of the chopper.

The Pave Hawk zoomed through the canyon. No one liked flying in this terrain. The mountains were steep and tree covered—plenty of places for bad guys to hide. And the Taliban liked nothing more than shooting down helicopters.

But when you were a PJ, a Pararescueman, you didn't get to pick the time and place. You went where you were sent—no matter the time or the place. Still, no one would choose the rugged terrain of Afghanistan.

"Airman, get that IV started," Sergeant "Mako" Marks said.

"I can't get a vein," Airman Bashir said through gritted teeth. He held the patient's arm.

"His blood pressure is dropping," Garcia said, "He's going to flat line!"

"Got it!" Bashir said. He sank the needle into the patient's inner arm. IV fluid flowed. He squeezed the IV bag, trying to make it go faster. The patient had been shot in the neck. The bullet had passed through, narrowly missing the spine. But there was still a lot of damage that needed treatment.

A few seconds passed.

"Blood pressure rising," Garcia said. "Blood pressure ninety over forty."

Mako took a deep breath. "That was way too close," he said.

The oxygen monitor beeped.

"What now?" Bashir asked.

"Oxygen levels dropping!" Garcia said.

"He's turning blue!" Mako said. "Check his airway!"

Before they could, the patient coughed. Then coughed again. His mouth was frothy with blood.

Bashir turned the patient's head to the side and pried open his mouth. "I've got blood!" Bashir said. He reached for a suction tube to try and clear the throat.

"No good!" Garcia said. "He's still struggling for air! The bullet may have collapsed his throat."

"He must be bleeding internally," Mako said. "Maybe a punctured lung. He'll drown in his own blood."

They worked quickly and efficiently. The suction was not effective. The patient's throat kept filling up with blood.

"Get the respirator," Mako said.

Bashir fitted the mask over the patient's nose and mouth.

"No good," Garcia said. "The oxygen isn't getting through."

"We're going to have to cric him!" Mako said.

"Seriously?" Bashir gulped.

A "cric" was a cricothyrotomy. Someone would have to cut through the throat tissue below the blockage and insert a tube. It would allow the patient to breathe.

"Do it, Bash!" Mako said. "Do it now!"

"I've never done one!" Bashir said. His voice was shaky. "Garcia should do it."

"Negative, Airman Bashir," Mako said. "You've got to cric this patient."

Bashir sat back on his haunches.

"Blood pressure falling again," Garcia said. "He needs air. We're losing him!"

Bashir pulled a scalpel and an alcohol wipe from the med kit. He swabbed the patient's throat with alcohol to sterilize it. He felt below the patient's Adam's apple, looking for the right spot. Then he carefully cut through the skin and into the esophagus.

"Tube!" Bashir said.

Garcia slapped a plastic tube in his hand. Bashir fitted it through the cut and into the airway. He was rewarded with a gasping breath from the patient.

"Good work, Bash!" Mako said.

"BP stabilizing. Oxygen levels rising," Garcia reported.

The tube whistled in the patient's throat. Bashir attached the oxygen line to it. The man's chest rose and fell. He could now breathe on his own.

"I could live with not having to do one of those ever again," Bashir said.

"That's how we roll, airman!" Mako said.

The chopper started its descent to the base. Once it landed, medical personnel rushed to it with a gurney. They removed the patient and sprinted toward the base hospital.

Bashir, Mako, and Garcia watched the man roll away. It was out of their hands now. It was up to the doctors to take care of him.

Lieutenant Jamal Jenkins, their CRO, strolled up to the group.

"That was good work, gentleman," Lieutenant Jenkins said. "Especially you, Bash. Great job."

Lieutenant Jenkins was a legend among PJs. Just over thirty years old, he had already been awarded a Distinguished Service Cross and two Purple Hearts. Bashir couldn't help but be proud at the compliment given by Jenkins.

"Thanks, Lieutenant," Bashir said. "It was a team effort on that Cat Alpha."

"Yes, it was. But you did especially well under pressure," Jenkins said.

"So, what's up, Loot?" Mako asked. "You don't usually come to greet us when we land."

"I came to tell you that you've got forty-five minutes to gather your gear," Jenkins said. "We have new orders. We're joining up with an international humanitarian relief effort in Dumar."

"The Dumar in Africa?" Mako asked.

"Correct," Jenkins said. "A dam failed, and there is massive flooding in the highlands. In addition to the flooding, there is a civil war in the country. Competing warlords with innocent people caught in the middle."

"There's going to be shooting," Garcia said.

"Most likely," Jenkins said.

"Nothing that frightens me," Mako said.

Jenkins chuckled. "Mako, remember, we shoot only if we have to."

"Of course," Mako said. "I always let the bad guys shoot first."

"It's hard to tell who the bad guy is a lot of the time," Garcia said.

"I hear you, Garcia," Jenkins said. "We're not going there to pick a side. We're going to help people."

"Roger that, Loot," Mako said. "We'll be ready."

They each pulled their gear out of the Pave Hawk and headed toward their quarters.

"Africa," Mako muttered. "I've never been to Africa."

"I hear it's nice this time of year," Jenkins said.

"Loot, for some reason I question the accuracy of your information," Mako said.

"That's probably a good idea," Jenkins said, smiling.

Forty-five minutes later, their plane took off from the base. It banked and turned east. Headed for Africa.

GLOSSARY

CAT ALPHA—Short for 'Category Alpha'. A category alpha patient is one that is seriously injured and requires immediate medical attention.

AFGHANISTAN—War-torn country in Southern Asia.

CONCUSSION— An injury to the brain caused by a hard blow to the head.

DIALECT—A form of a language that is spoken in a particular area or by a particular group of people.

FORWARD OPERATING BASE—A secured military position, such as a military base, that is used for tactical operation support.

GOLDEN HOUR—When a patient has been wounded or injured, the first hour after the injury happens is the Golden Hour. Patients who can reach a hospital for treatment within the Golden Hour have far better chances of surviving their injury.

PAVE HAWK—The Sikorsky HH-60 helicopter, the primary craft used by PJs.

PEDROS—A nickname for PJs, from the helicopter call sign of Pedro 1 and Pedro 2 which is used on combat missions.

RESPIRATOR— A device worn over the mouth or nose that cleans the air so a person can breathe safely.

INFORMATION BRIEFING:

AFGHANISTAN

○ Location: South and Central Asia

○ Population: Nearly 36 million people

○ Name History: Afghanistan means "Land of the Pashtuns." The Pashtuns are an Iranic ethnic group.

WIND AND SAND

Loose sand in the desert is the primary cause of sandstorms. Strong wind picks up the dirt and causes poor visibility. The heated air of the desert creates the storms, which can be hundreds of miles in diameter. Afghanis wear scarves to keep the sand from their eyes and face. Afghanistan is a mountainous country. The mountain terrain is rugged. Most Afghanis live in the mountain valleys. Farming is the largest occupation in Afghanistan.

ABOUT THE AUTHOR

Michael P. Spradlin is the *New York Times* bestselling author of more than thirty books for children and adults. His books include the international bestselling trilogy *The Youngest Templar*, the Edgar nominated *Spy Goddess* series and the Wrangler Award Winning *Off Like the Wind: The First Ride of the Pony Express*. He lives in Lapeer, Michigan. Visit his website at www.michaelspradlin.com.

ABOUT THE ILLUSTRATOR

Spiros Karkavelas is a concept artist and photographer based in Greece. He graduated from Feng Zhu School of Design in Singapore in 2013 and has done work with various video game and book publishing companies. His realistic illustrations often have a theme of modern-day or futuristic warfare, and he draws inspiration from true war stories, the realities of the battlefield, and how war brings out both the worst and best in human nature.

DISCUSSION QUESTIONS

1. PJs have to be aware of the Golden Hour when recovering injured patients. How do you think they keep their focus while treating their patients and tracking how much time they have to get them to the base hospital?

2. During the mission, Mako makes soldiers from other branches into honorary PJs. Research the different United States Military groups and think about the story. What similarities do the soldiers and PJs have? How are they different?

3. The PJs have to be prepared to help any injured, even one of their own. During Sandstorm Blast, Jenkins is hurt and George has to carry him through the battle. Imagine you are George while carrying Jenkins in a combat zone. How do you think you'd react?

WRITING PROMPTS

1. The sand in desert locales is very tough on equipment. Pretend you are on a PJ mission and a sandstorm blows in. What steps would you take to make it through the storm?

2. The desert is hot during the daytime and freezing cold at night. If you were stranded in the desert, how would keep your patients warm without using a fire that might attract enemy attention?

3. The PJs risk their lives to save people in horrible situations. Their motto is "These things we do so others may live." Write a story where you are the PJ risking your own life to save someone else.

FOLLOW EACH HEROIC MISSION OF
PARARESCUE CORPS

DENALI
STORM

NILE
CHAOS

SANDSTORM
BLAST

VIPER
STRIKE

Find cool websites and more books like this
one at **www.facthound.com**.

Just type in the Book ID: 9781496551597
and you're ready to go!